THE BAD SEED

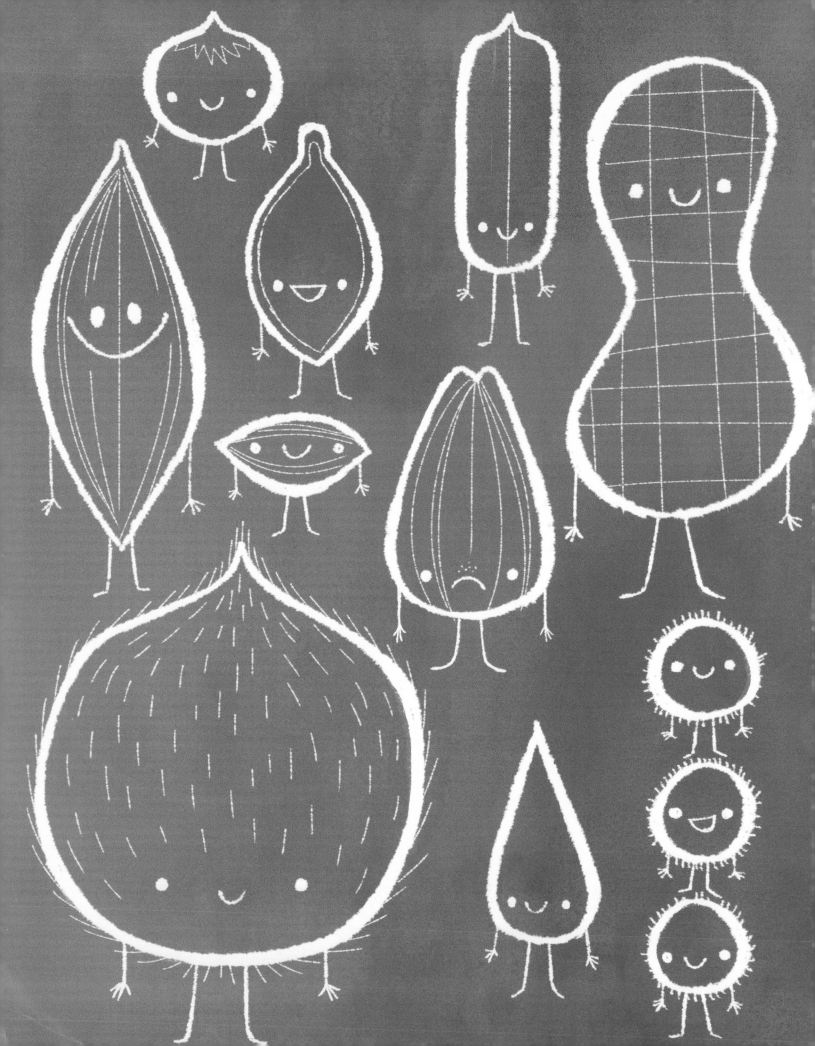

To Jono, Jodi, Lily, and Oren
—J.J.

Dedicated to the baddest seeds I know:
Vincent and William
—P.O.

ISBN 978-1-338-54198-4

Text copyright © 2017 by Jory John. Illustrations copyright © 2017 by Pete Oswald.
All rights reserved. Published by Scholastic Inc., 557 Broadway, New York, NY 10012,
by arrangement with HarperCollins Children's Books, a division of HarperCollins Publishers.
SCHOLASTIC and associated logos are trademarks and/or registered trademarks of Scholastic Inc.

12 11 10 9 8 7 6 5 4   20 21 22 23 24

Printed in the U.S.A.   40

This edition first printing, January 2019

The artist used scanned watercolor textures and digital paint to create the illustrations for this book.
Typography by Jeanne L. Hogle

THE BAD SEED

written by JORY JOHN • illustrations by PETE OSWALD

SCHOLASTIC INC.

I'm a bad seed.

A baaaaaaaaaad seed.

Oh yeah. It's true.

The other seeds, they look at me, and they say,

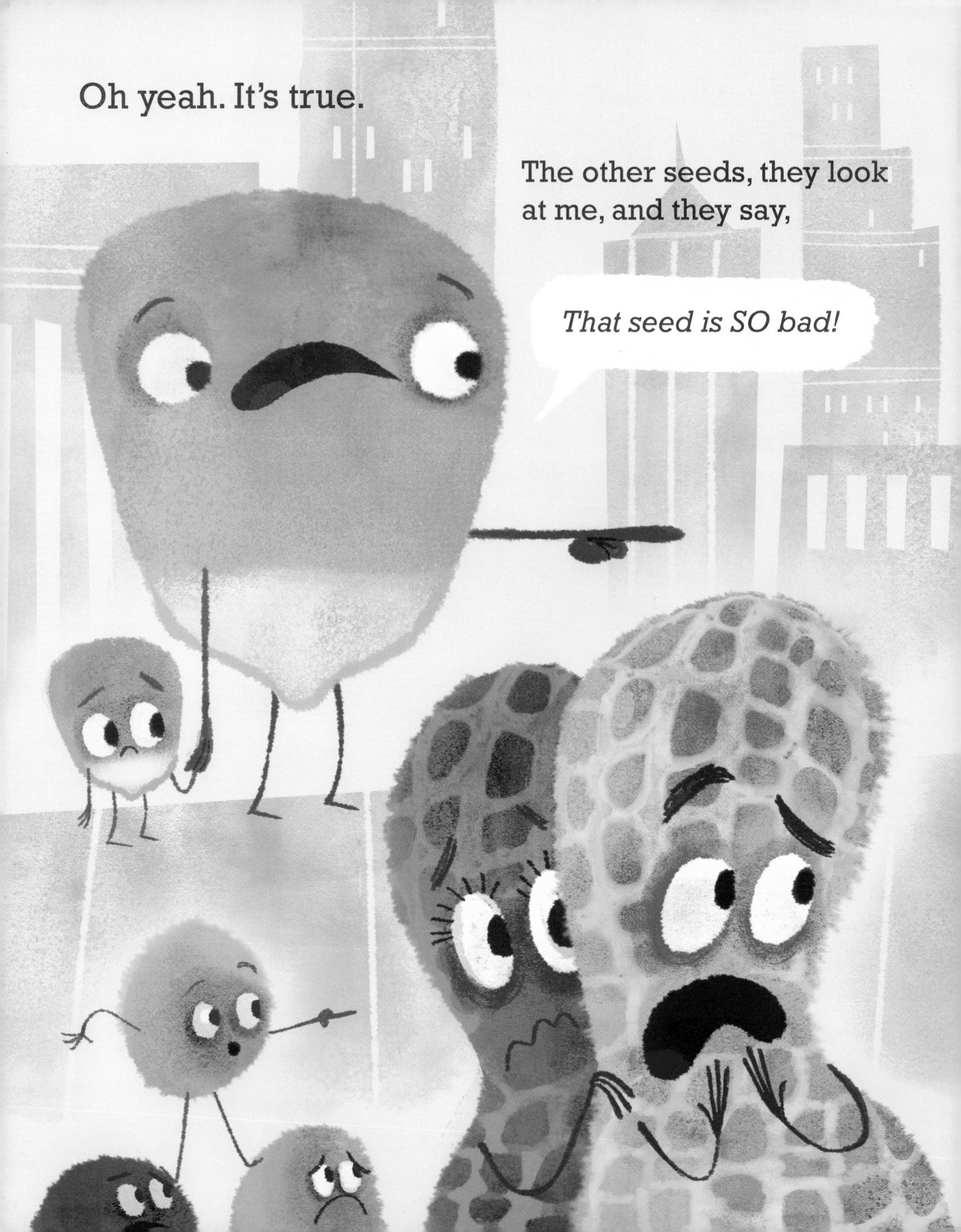

When they think I'm not listening, they mumble,

There goes a baaaad seed.

But I can hear them. I have good hearing for a seed.

How bad am I?

You really want to know?

Well ...

I never put things back where they belong.

I'm late to everything.

I tell long jokes with
no punch lines.

I never wash my hands.   Or my feet.

I lie about pointless stuff.

I cut in line. Every time.

I stare at everybody.   I glare at everybody.

I finish everybody's sentences. And I never listen.

And I do *lots* of other bad things, too.
Know why? Because I'm a bad seed.

A baaaaaaaaaaad seed.

I just can't help it.

Sure, I wasn't *always* this bad.
I was born a humble seed, on a simple sunflower,
in an unremarkable field.

I had a big family.
Seeds everywhere.
We found ways of having fun.
We were close.

But then the petals dropped.

And our flower drooped.

It's kind of a blur.

fresh

SUNFLOWER SEEDS

DELICIOUS

I remember a bag. . . .

Everything went dark . . .

. . . and then . . . *then* . . .

. . . a giant!

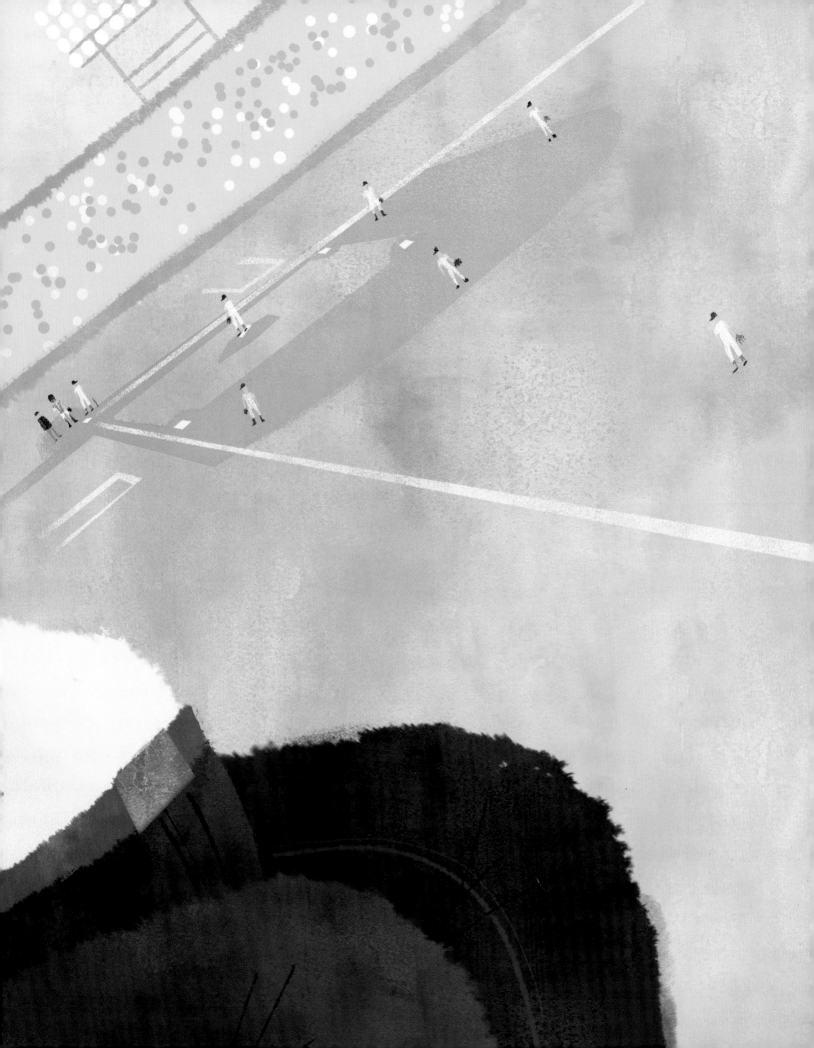

I thought I was a goner. . . .
I thought I was done for. . . .
I screamed and I hollered. . . .

AHHHHHHHHH!

"PTOOOOOOOOOOO!"

But I was spit out at the last possible second.

I flew through the air, and I landed
under the bleachers with
a huge thud.

THUD!

When I woke up, it was dark outside.
A wad of gum had softened my fall.
I felt OK. But something had changed in me.
I'd become a different seed entirely.

I'd become a bad seed.

A baaaaaaaaaad seed.

That's right.
I stopped smiling.
I kept to myself.
I drifted.

I was friend to nobody
and bad to everybody.
I was lost on purpose.
I lived inside a soda can.

I didn't care.
And it suited me.

Until recently.

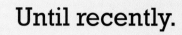

I've made a big decision.
I've decided I don't want to be
a bad seed anymore.
I'm ready to be happy.

It's hard to be good when
you're so used to being bad.
But I'm trying.
I'm taking it one day at a time.

Sure, I still forget to listen.

And I still show up late.

And I still talk during movies. And I do all kinds of other bad stuff.

But I also say thank you.

And I say please. And I smile.

And I hold doors open for people.
Not always. But sometimes.

And even though I still feel bad, sometimes,
I also feel kind of good.
It's sort of a mix.

All I can do is keep trying.
And keep thinking,
Maybe I'm not such a bad seed after all.

Hey, look, there goes that bad seed. . . .
Actually, he's not all that bad anymore.

I heard that.

JORY JOHN is a *New York Times* bestselling author and two-time E. B. White Read Aloud Honor recipient. Jory's work includes the award-winning Goodnight Already! series; the bestselling Terrible Two series; the recent picture books *Penguin Problems* and *Quit Calling Me a Monster!*; and the national bestseller *All My Friends Are Dead*, among many other books. He lives and works in Oregon, where he tries to be a very good seed, indeed.

PETE OSWALD is a painter, illustrator, and filmmaker. He is the cocreator of *Mingo the Flamingo.* Pete worked as a character designer and concept artist on the popular films *Madagascar: Escape 2 Africa, Cloudy with a Chance of Meatballs,* and *Hotel Transylvania.* His short film *The Story of Walls* earned him an Annie Award nomination. He was the production designer of *The Angry Birds Movie.* Pete lives in Santa Monica, California, with his wife and two sons.